For Sandy, Becca and Sarah

Crumps Barn Studio
Crumps Barn, Syde, Cheltenham GL53 9PN
www.crumpsbarnstudio.co.uk

Text and illustrations © Mike Mogg 2021

First printed 2021

The rights of Mike Mogg to be identified as the author and illustrator of this work has been asserted by him in accordance with the Copyright, Designs and Patents Act 1988.

All rights reserved. No part of this publication may be reproduced, stored in a retrieval system, or transmitted in any form or by any means, electronic, mechanical, photocopying, recording or otherwise, without the prior permission of the copyright owner.

Typeset in Apertura

Printed in Gloucestershire on FSC certified paper by SevernPrint, a carbon neutral company

ISBN 978-1-8382298-5-6

the fantastic world of CracKoNoLa

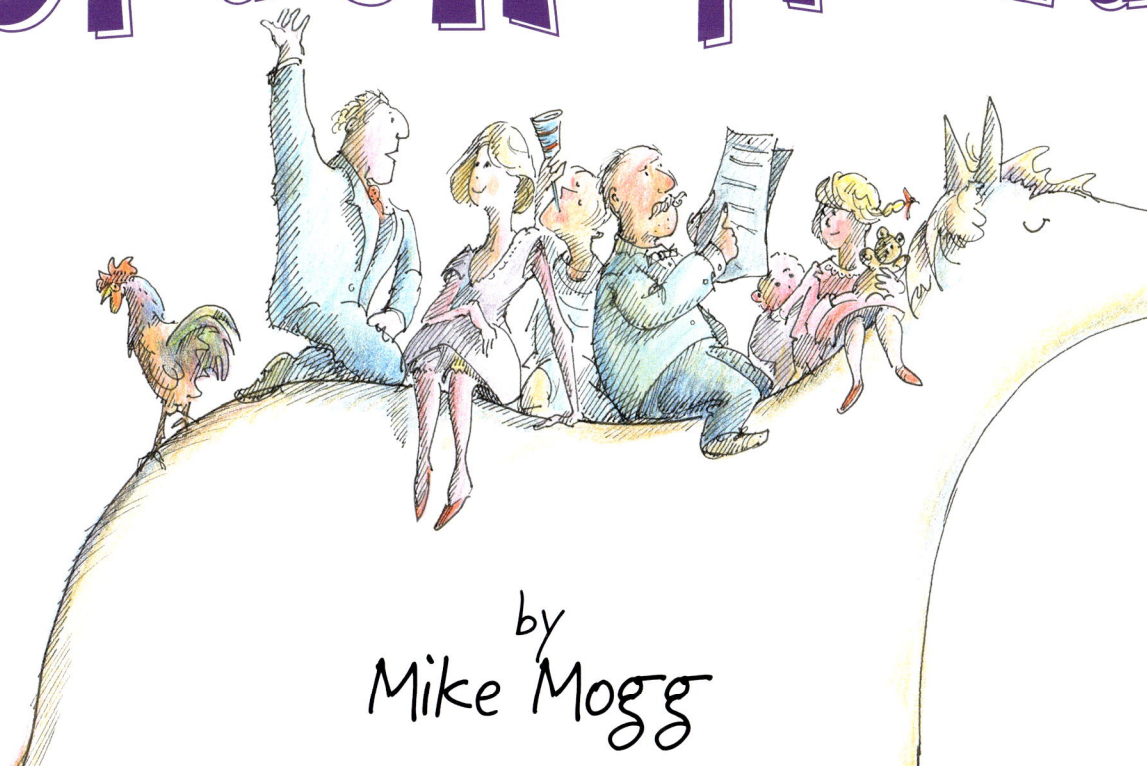

by Mike Mogg

There was a clock who lost his tock!
He could tick a bit (which he did a lot)
Like this:

Tic – tic – tic – tic – tic – tic – tic – tic –

Grandfather Clock was really quite shocked.
Slowly and seriously, he loudly

TOCKED!

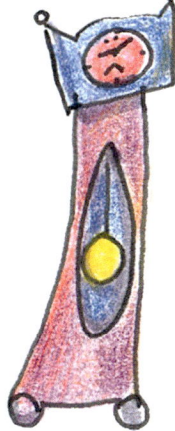

The little alarm **'Pinged'** and started to ring:

R...r...r...r...r...r...r...r...rrrrrrrrrrrrrr...ING!!

Every watch in the place
tried to keep up the pace.
But without any tock ...

They just couldn't

STOP!

Little Bertie, on his birthday,
said, "Dear Mum, I feel quite thirsty.
I'm rather tired of squash and tea
and as the day belongs to me
I really fancy fizzy pop …
with lots of ice cream piled on top!"

Said Mum: "Let's visit Giovanni's shop!"

Giovanni, with a grin,
embraced them both and took them in,
enquired of Mum, "What kind of flavour?
There are so many sorts to savour!

"Chocolate Fudge or plain Vanilla,
Rum and Raisin, Caramella,
Strawberry Bon-Bons, Lemon Pieces …
Anything that really pleases!"

Bertie's little eyes grew rounder,
smiled and said with youthful candour,
"I cannot choose, I'm in a spot
I think I'll have to **take the LOT!**"

Mother wondered was that wise,
then closed her eyes and gently sighed.

Now as you know, or perhaps you don't –
Ice Cream dropped in Soda floats!
Like icebergs drifting in the ocean
the fizzing sets them all in motion.

(normally it doesn't matter –
you can take your time, perhaps have a natter)
BUT over-fill the frothing glass,
you set up movements of a different CLASS!

Bertie really didn't care,
he stirred in more than most would dare.
Then demanded even MORE!!!!!
The multicoloured gaseous goo,
took on a terrifying hue,
changing from red to green then blue –
like thunder clouds it grew and grew!

Ice Cream spread across the floor
oozing from the shop's front door,
this sugary wave of freezing splendour
made July seem more like December!
It stretched as far as you could see,
it covered every house and tree ...

Then with one enormous 'POP'
it hurled poor Bertie from the shop!

People came from miles around,
to marvel at this snowy land.
They skied and sledged and many skated,
everyone felt quite elated!

Polar Bears then came on tour,
they laughed so much it made them roar.
But of Bertie there was no sign …
And all his friends began to pine.

Mother said, "how shall we cope?
We really mustn't give up hope."

Father said they shouldn't wait
and really must investigate!

He advertised for old explorers,
people used to giving orders,
who knew exactly what to do
with igloos, ice picks and canoes!

They came in crowds by bus and train,
hairy men who didn't complain,
intrepid men in dark blue glasses,
used to dealing with crevasses,
determined they would give a hand
to tame this new-found Ice Cream Land!

They scoured the coloured frozen wastes,
searched all the ice that filled the place,
when after months and months of tracking,
Little Bertie was discovered napping
On a block of Strawberry Ice!

With shouts of triumph and homeward bound
they told his parents he was found!
The family Doctor quickly called –
said Bertie should be slowly thawed.

Keep him cool and wait for summer.
No creamy drinks, they'll make him shudder,
nor anything that's cold and fizzy –
it's guaranteed to make him dizzy!
Keep him quiet, lots of naps,
drink only water from the tap …

Bertie is much better now,
but never tires of telling people:

PLEASE keep your Ice Cream Soda SIMPLE!

Snails are sneaky, that's to say,
they slimily eat my greens away.

There was a flower upon my lawn,
I noticed that today it's 'gawn'...

My cat is black
He doesn't scratch
In fact – he doesn't do-a-lot
(or catch-a-lot)

He does however sleep-a-lot
In chairs, on stairs, or beds and drawers
He loves any sunny patch-a-lot
We call him Mr Cat-nap-a-lot
(or Katnap for short)

Oh Please
Don't tease!
Elephants don't hide in trees!
If they should sneeze,
the breeze
would blow the leaves away!
Their trunks would freeze
They would wheeze!

It's no disguise
They cannot hide!
They're far too fat and high and wide!
Better if they stand around
Firmly fixed upon the ground
Trying not to make a sound.
No one then will notice them.

Here comes Freddie FEROCIOUS, a mouth full of plums,
black leather gloves without any thumbs.
A large stripy pillow
tied round his middle,
a newspaper hat,
a bow from a fiddle.
He looks very fierce, and I've heard he has said –
he keeps a large monster locked up in the shed.

Freddie Ferocious keep quiet – please Do!
You'll upset *my* Monster, he's bigger than you!
He's got six orange legs and twenty-four feet.
You may be my brother, but he'd love you to EAT!
He has very bad breath and teeth that are Yellow.
So, give me a plum or he might start to

BELLOW!

The Vac-u-um doth hum
and picketh up each tiny crumb.
It beateth in the morning air
extracting every *minute* hair.
Its burbles cause much turbulence!
My head it **FILLS**,
the carpet kills –
it sucks its frills!
I may require an ambulance!

Are You coming to see US,
Or are WE going to visit YOU?

So ... why all the fuss, there is a bus!
tho if it should rain, I may take the train.
But an unfussable bus is really a must
and not any tougher than an old fashioned puffer!
That's a Dragon on wheels, with a wagon for meals,
a whistle, a bell, a cindery smell!

If I don't take the train I may try a plane:
there's no queuing or pushing,
they give you a cushion, a seat to relax in.
I did think of a bike, maybe a trike,
an elegant scooter complete with a hooter!

I suppose that a boat would keep us afloat,
but not one with oars as they can be bores,
there's far too much rowing, all that to-ing and fro-ing,
and not very fast, perhaps with a mast –
I'd quite like a sail, we might see a whale!

A horse with a cart would be quite a big lark –
clipping and clopping, without need for stopping,
and always plenty of room for the shopping.
Don't come in the car, it's really too far
and you'll end up all smelly from petrol and tar!

But first ... are WE coming to see YOU,
Or are YOU going to visit US?

Gerald loved his trumpet
it was twice as big as him
but with every breath it took to blow,
it almost sucked him in!

He blew ... it sucked!
It wouldn't let him go –
"It's eating me!" the young chap said,
as his feet began to glow.

"It's taken all my breath away,
my tonsils have turned yellow –
I'm really lost for words," he sighed,
but the trumpet gave a

BELLOW!

(It took a sweep near on a week,
to save the little fellow!)

"I'm going to join the Circus"
That's what sister Sally said.
"So I'll need a pretty pony and
feathers to wear on my head!
I shall be a bareback rider –
World Famous!" is what Sally said.

We'll jump through hoops,
and dangle from loops,
soar through the air with never a care!
When the audience gasps and closes its eyes –
we'll jump from the ring and to their surprise ...
do three double somersaults
to make them all smile!

After the show when everyone cheers,
we'll sign all their programmes and then disappear
to a comfortable bunk in a red caravan,
there'll be lots of iced biscuits, gifts from the fans!

"I'm going to join the Circus"
That's what sister Sally said!

How big is BIG?
How small is small?
How do you know if
you're short,
or you're tall?

When you are little
everything's bigger!
When you grow taller
is everything smaller?

Ancient sailors
make poor tailors

Although, of course
(and very fitting) –

They are extremely
good at knitting.

Millie loves her marmalade
but to her mum's dismay,
she spoons it with the garden spade …
and spreads it on the balustrade!

Granny plays for England
She also has a drum!
Granny has a grasshopper
She rides it just for fun.

Granny likes to sing and dance,
so does Granny's cat!
They've both appeared upon TV,
and what do you think of that –
The town gave her a medal,
the cat received a rat!

Grandpa smells of peppermints
and has a little cough.
he likes to flutter out at night
riding on a moth!

Because of Granny's drumming
and the singing of the cat,
he stays upstairs for days and days
making earmuffs for the rat!

Beetles and Bugs
Beetles and Bugs
I don't mind Snails
I'm not one for Slugs!

(ok, look I'm a slug, alright?
We have to wear these things –
I live on a building site ...
I'm not a SNAIL!)

Harold's headache's getting **WORSE**
He feels his head is fit to burst!
The party's going with a swing
but perhaps they could try *whispering?*
He didn't ask for them to call,
it was HIS party after all!
They've eaten all the cake and jelly,
spilt cola on his nice new telly!
Next year he intends to try
birthdaying quietly in Paraguay!

THE END